The Dreaded
Snowman Wedgie

Charlie Bacon

The Dreaded Snowman Wedgie

by Gary Hogg

ILLUSTRATED BY ELISE SUMMERS

Little Buckaroo Books

Text copyright © 2015 by Gary Hogg
Illustrations copyright © by Elise Summers
Designed by Matt Shay
ISBN 978-0-93077-140-9

Printed in the U.S.A.

10 9 8 7 6 5 4 3 2 1

To four of the bravest people I know,

Ryan Blount

Summer Kinkade

T. J. Hopkins

Keygan Wright

Contents

Chapter 1

Now I Have to Get New Teeth

Charlie Bacon opened his mouth and let the snowflakes collect on his tongue. He loved the taste of winter. Flopping onto his back, he made his first snow angel of the year.

"What are you doing?" shouted his mom from the open back door. "You're in your pajamas! Come in for breakfast."

"Just one more," replied Charlie, moving to his left and making a brother for the first angel. As he sat up, a snowball crashed into the back of his head. He turned around just in time to see his sister, Shrudi, launch a second snowball. This one hit Charlie in the forehead.

He wasn't an angel anymore. Charlie went into full attack mode. He quickly pulled together a snowball and threw it at his sister.

"Missed me, missed me, now you have to kiss me," shouted Shrudi as she headed for the back door.

"No way," yelled Charlie, scooping up a monster-sized snowball. "I never miss twice." He reared back like a big league pitcher and threw the icy ball as hard as he could. At that moment, Mom opened the back door to see why Charlie hadn't come in yet. Shrudi ducked and the snowball hit Charlie's mom directly in the face.

Everyone froze. Mom thawed out first. She shut the door and both kids heard the lock click. "This is your fault!" shouted Charlie.

"You threw the snowball," snapped Shrudi.

"You threw the first one!" yelled Charlie.

They were still arguing when the back door swung open. Mom was wearing her winter coat and gloves.

"Uh oh," said Charlie. "It's a snow war." He tried to make a quick snowball but by the time he stood up to throw it, Mom blasted him with two rapid-fire ice balls.

Shrudi was laughing when a snowball hit her in the mouth. Mom was a snowball throwing machine.

"Run!" shouted Charlie as two more snowballs exploded on his back. When Shrudi raced for the door, she was plastered by three fast snowballs. She tripped and landed face-first in the freezing snow.

"We give up!" shouted Charlie, holding up his hands. "You win. Where'd you learn to throw like that?"

"I grew up with four brothers, but not one of them ever beat me in a snowball fight," answered Mom.

As soon as they were in the house, Mom ordered the kids to dry off and dress for school. "Can I have a hot bath?" asked Charlie. "I'm freezing."

"Of course, but you don't have a lot of time," said Mom.

"Do I have time to eat some chili beans first?" asked Charlie. "I like to make my own Jacuzzi bubbles."

"No bubbles," said Mom.

By the time Charlie got to the bathroom, Shrudi was already taking a shower. Charlie pounded on the door and yelled, "Don't use all the hot water!"

Shrudi was a hot-water hog, so Charlie knew his bath would have to wait. He pulled off his wet PJs and left them in the hall. He hurried into his room and dressed himself in jeans and a sweatshirt. He pulled on the cleanest dirty socks he could find and raced to the kitchen for breakfast.

Charlie was almost done eating a bowl of oatmeal when the doorbell rang. He popped his head around the corner to see his best friend, Biff, dressed head to toe in brand new snow clothes. "Hurry up," said Biff.

"I've got to go," said Charlie to his mom.

"Brush your teeth," ordered Mom.

Charlie busted into the bathroom. Shrudi was still in the shower and she started screaming like a police siren. "GET OUT! GET OUT! GET OUT! MOM! MOM! MOM!"

Charlie ignored the screams and grabbed a toothbrush. After squirting some toothpaste on it, he shoved it in his mouth. Shrudi's head poked out from behind the shower curtain.

"You idiot, that's mine," she wailed. "Now I have to get a new toothbrush."

"Now I have to get new teeth," said Charlie, spitting into the sink.

Charlie left the drama of the bathroom behind. "Bye, Mom," he shouted as he pulled on his coat and followed Biff out the front door.

Chapter 2
Artsy Fartsy

When the boys got to Central Elementary, Charlie plopped down next to the flagpole and made a snow angel in the fresh snow.

"Why do you like snow angels so much?" asked Biff.

"Grandma said snow angels bring you good luck," said Charlie.

Biff flopped in the snow next to Charlie and made some good luck of his own. The boys were still waving their arms in the snow when the bell rang.

Charlie and Biff dusted themselves off and hurried into the school. When they walked into Room 7,

Mr. Beecher was writing the day's schedule on the whiteboard. Charlie quickly read the day's events. "What does Artist in Residence mean?" he asked.

"That's very exciting news. I'll fill you in on all the details after morning announcements," said Mr. Beecher.

Allison couldn't wait until after morning announcements. "Are we going to visit an artist's house?" she asked.

Mr. Beecher turned to Allison and said, "Patience is a virtue."

"I'm an expert on patience," said Allison. "My mom says I'm always testing her patience."

"That's not a good thing," said Rayce.

"It is too," argued Allison. "To give a test you have to know the answers."

"But you're not giving a test, you are the test," said Rayce.

Mr. Beecher tried to hide his smile as he called the class to order. "Speaking of tests, I hope you all studied your spelling words last night."

"P-a-t-e-i-n-c-e," spelled Allison. "For all you bad spellers I just spelled the word patience."

"Misspelled, you mean," said Biff. "It's i before e."

Allison's face turned eraser red, and Dr. Brown's voice came over the intercom. After the Pledge of Allegiance, he read the morning announcements. The last item of business was big news. "Nationally known artist Sarah Harper will be spending the week at our school as artist in residence. She will be working with all of the students during her time here. Friday night we will be having an art show where we will be highlighting some of the best art created during the week."

"I'm going to create a self-portrait," announced Allison. "When people at the art show see it they will. . ."

"Run away screaming," interrupted Tony.

Before anyone could laugh, Mr. Beecher cleared his throat and glared at Tony.

"Sorry," said Tony.

"I knew you'd have lots of questions so I downloaded a short video about Mrs. Harper from the Internet," said Mr. Beecher. "She's a fascinating person."

The students were mesmerized by the video. Sarah Harper had lived all over the world studying and creating art.

"She's pretty," said Shelby.

"She paints like an angel," added Charlie.

"We're meeting with her right after lunch," said Mr. Beecher. "This is a fantastic opportunity to learn from a master. I expect you all to be on your best behavior."

When Charlie entered the cafeteria for lunch, he noticed a group of students gathered around a table in the back of the lunchroom. Charlie got a tray and pushed it down the counter to get his food. His dad was the school cook and today he was serving his famous smack and cheese.

Charlie's dad smiled as he scooped the creamy

noodles onto Charlie's tray. "Who's over there?" asked Charlie, looking at the crowded table.

"That's Sarah Harper," said Dad.

"She's famous," said Charlie. "We saw a video about her."

Dad leaned toward Charlie and whispered, "She's artsy-fartsy if you ask me. She wouldn't even try my smack and cheese. She had Dr. Brown bring in a gourmet meal from Café Francois."

Charlie took his food and sat between Biff and Rayce. Biff was slurping down his lunch. "Why does your dad call this smack and cheese?" asked Biff between bites.

"It's so good you smack your lips when you eat it," explained Charlie.

"Now I get it," said Biff. He smacked his lips and took another huge bite of noodles.

"I can't wait until Sarah Harper visits our room," said Rayce.

Charlie looked both ways and motioned for the boys to come close. "Dad says she is artsy-fartsy," whispered Charlie.

"Does that mean what I think it means?" asked Rayce.

"Fancy farts," said Biff as he started giggling uncontrollably.

"Do they smell fancy or sound fancy?" asked Rayce between fits of laughter. The boys were laughing so loud that Dr. Brown came over to their table. All three boys tried to stop laughing but failed.

"You need to hold it down over here," he said.

The boys finally got control of their laughter and Charlie said, "We'll be quiet."

"Good," said the principal. "You sounded like you

were on laughing gas."

When they heard Dr. Brown say, "laughing gas," they all started giggling again.

"I'm guessing this hilarity has something to do with gas," said Dr. Brown. The boys laughed harder and shook their heads in agreement. "I think you should clean your trays and head to the playground. One of the reasons we have art week is to class up the school a little bit. This kind of behavior is unacceptable."

"Yes, sir," said the boys as they jumped up and took their trays to the dish washer.

As soon as they were outside, Rayce did his best Dr. Brown impersonation, "One of the reasons we have fart week is to gas up the school a little bit." The boys were still laughing when the bell rang.

Chapter 3

It's Really Disgusting

Allison had completed three self-portraits and taped them to the front of her desk by the time Sarah Harper walked into Room 7. She was a tall lady and her head was topped by a blossom of curly blonde hair. She was carrying what looked like a humongous briefcase, which she placed on Mr. Beecher's desk.

"What's in the huge case?" asked Tony.

"In a video about you we saw a painting of an elephant," said Rayce. "Was the elephant real?"

Mr. Beecher held up his hand. "Class, there will be time for questions later. For now, let's give our undivided attention to Mrs. Harper."

Sarah Harper smiled and Charlie felt she was looking right at him. It was his first time meeting a real artist and even if she had a gas problem he was impressed.

"I'll answer your questions later. First, I have some questions for you. Does anyone know what art is?"

Allison raised her hand and cleared her throat extra loud for extra attention. When Mrs. Harper pointed to her, Allison announced, "My name is Allison. I am an artist too. These are some of my most recent self-portraits. I could be your assistant this week and help teach the classes."

"Thank you for the offer but I think I can manage," replied Sarah Harper. She repeated her question, "Does anyone know what art is?"

Rayce raised his hand, "Is it drawing pictures?"

"It can be," answered Mrs. Harper.

"Statues are art," added Shelby.

"Sometimes," said Mrs. Harper.

"Art makes you feel," blurted Charlie, without raising his hand.

Sarah Harper's face brightened. "What's your name?" she asked.

"Charlie Bacon," answered Charlie.

"Well, Mr. Bacon, you're exactly right. Art comes from the heart. The artist hopes to make a creation that causes people to feel something," she explained.

She took a painting of an elephant out of her art portfolio and held it up for the class to see. "This is Taj. I painted his portrait while on a trip to Thailand. How does my painting of Taj make you feel?"

"Happy," said Shelby. "I like elephants."

Rhonda raised her hand and said, "It makes me feel sad. There's a chain around his foot."

Charlie studied the picture and raised his hand. "It makes me feel hopeful. When I look in his eye I see courage, and where there is courage, there is hope."

"Wonderful! You have an eye for details," said Mrs. Harper. "Artists notice the little things that others miss. Where did you learn that where there is courage, there is hope?"

"From my grandma," said Charlie. "She says it takes a lot of courage to be married to my grandpa, but she hopes it's worth it."

Mrs. Harper laughed as she took a laptop computer out of her briefcase and connected it to the projector. For the next thirty minutes she taught the students about some of the great artists throughout time. She showed art work from Picasso, Rembrandt, Leonardo Da Vinci, Raphael, and Michelangelo. She explained the use of color, proportion, and movement in art. By the time she had finished, the students were excited to make their own art projects.

"Each of you will be creating a painting or statue this week," concluded Mrs. Harper. "You will need to get started on your art project right away. I will meet with your class again later this week to advise and hopefully inspire you. On Friday evening we will have an art show. The name of this year's show is A Celebration of Inspiration."

After Sarah Harper left, Mr. Beecher gave the students some time to work on ideas for their art projects. While the other students headed to the supply closet to get paper and crayons, Charlie grabbed a box of modeling clay. If Michelangelo, the greatest artist of all time, made statues so would he.

Charlie broke off a huge piece of the stone-colored clay and rolled it between his hands to soften it. "Does anyone have a mirror?" he asked.

Allison pulled a princess hand mirror out of her desk and handed it to Charlie. "If you break this mirror, you owe me twenty dollars and I do not take checks," warned Allison.

Charlie studied his face in the mirror and then began sculpting. He pinched and pulled, smashed and smushed until his face appeared in the clay. Biff passed by and said, "Cool monster. It's really disgusting."

Charlie quickly smoothed out the clay and returned the mirror to Allison. Creating a masterpiece was going to be harder than he thought.

Chapter 4

Michelangelo Never Had to Clean Toilets

Charlie's mom had a mug of hot chocolate waiting for Charlie when he got home. "How was your day?" she asked, handing Charlie the cocoa.

"Sarah Harper told me I have the heart of an artist," said Charlie.

"Who's Sarah Harper?" asked Mom.

"A famous artist," said Charlie. "She told me that I can see things that others can't."

"That's funny," said Mom. "You didn't manage to see that your room is a mess."

"I'm an artist not a maid," said Charlie. "I have more important things to consider."

"Maybe you should consider being grounded," said Mom.

"OK, I'll clean my room. Then can I go to Biff's house?" asked Charlie.

"If it passes inspection," said Mom.

After finishing his cocoa, Charlie hurried to his room. It was a disaster zone. He opened the window and left it open while he headed to the garage to get his favorite cleaning tools, a shovel and rake. His mom didn't understand the value of garden tools in housecleaning so he had to sneak them in.

In the garage, Charlie grabbed the shovel but dropped it when he spotted something better. He remembered how excited his dad was when he purchased the new leaf blower. "Son, watch and learn," his dad had said when he brought the blower home. "This is the Leaf Blaster 5000. It's the most powerful leaf blower known to man. This baby will make short work of a long job."

Dad had put on safety goggles and revved the Leaf Blaster 5000 like a hot rod before attacking the yard. Charlie had watched in amazement as the blower cleared their yard of every last leaf.

Charlie grabbed the safety goggles and picked up the Leaf Blaster 5000. He went around the house and pushed them though his open bedroom window. He zipped back around the house and raced through the back door.

Back in his room, Charlie placed the goggles over his eyes and gripped the handle of the pull rope that started the blower. After three hard yanks, a cloud of smoke coughed out of the exhaust and the Leaf Blaster 5000 roared to life.

Charlie put the harness over his shoulders and picked up the leaf blower. It sounded a lot louder than Charlie remembered. He pointed it at the pile of clothes on the floor and revved the engine wide open. The force of the Leaf Blaster shot the dirty clothes up in the air and they flew out the open window.

Then like a tornado, Charlie spun in a circle. The roaring wind from the Leaf Blaster picked up everything that wasn't nailed down. Underwear swirled in the air, action figures flew across the room, and candy wrappers fluttered like wild humming birds.

Charlie's mind whirled as the wind whipped the garbage around his room. He would never complain about cleaning ever again. The roar of the engine was so loud he didn't hear the screams of his mother as she charged down the hall. When the door flew open, Charlie pointed the leaf blower straight at his mom. The blast of wind almost knocked her over.

"Turn it off!" she shrieked.

"I can't hear you," shouted Charlie, still pointing the Leaf Blaster 5000 directly in his mom's face. Mom dropped her head and charged into the gust of wind like a linebacker on a football team.

When she got close enough, she flipped the switch to off. The Leaf Blaster 5000 sputtered to a stop. "What on earth are you doing!" yelled Mom.

"Cleaning my room the modern way," answered Charlie calmly.

Mom let out a huge sigh and said, "Go put this contraption back in the garage and clean your room the old-fashioned way."

"You mean the dumb slow way that will take forever," said Charlie.

"Yes the dumb slow way that will take forever," repeated Mom. "And don't forget to make your bed."

After Charlie returned the Leaf Blaster 5000 he noticed his bedroom window was still open. He looked out at the clothes that were piled on the snow. He knew he'd have to go outside and get them sooner or later. He decided on later and tossed the rest of the toys and clothes out the window as well. He made his bed and closed the window.

Charlie raced into the kitchen where his mom was

reading a magazine. He clicked his heels together, stood at attention and saluted. "Ready for inspection, sir," he announced.

"Already?" questioned Mom.

"See for yourself," said Charlie, heading to his room.

"I'm impressed," said Mom, giving the room the once-over. "You did a great job."

"All of us great artists have an eye for detail," bragged Charlie.

Charlie's mom gazed out the window and said, "It looks like it might snow." When she moved toward the window to get a better view, Charlie raced in front of her.

"Can I have some more hot chocolate?" he asked, trying to change the subject.

"I think one mug is plenty," said Mom swerving past Charlie on her way to the window. Charlie bounced to his left to stay in front of her.

"What are you doing?" asked Mom.

"Just admiring how pretty you are," said Charlie. "Will you pose for me so I can paint your portrait for the art show?" He grabbed Mom's arm and tried to lead her out of his room. "We need to go into the kitchen where the lighting is better."

Mom pulled her arm from Charlie's grip and stepped over to the window. She stared at the pile of clothes and garbage that was scattered in the yard.

"I wonder how those got out there?" asked Charlie.

Mom took a deep breath and slowly exhaled. "There are no shortcuts for doing the right thing," she said.

"I'll clean it all up," said Charlie.

"I know you will," said Mom. "And then you'll clean the bathroom, including scrubbing the toilet. It might inspire you."

Cleaning a toilet was not the inspiration Charlie was looking for. "I'll bet Michelangelo never had to clean toilets," complained Charlie.

"I'll bet Michelangelo kept his room clean," said Mom. By the time Charlie was done with cleaning the bathroom, it was suppertime.

Chapter 5

No Way!
No How!

The next morning, Charlie got a ride to school with his dad. "What's up?" asked Dad on the way to school. "You usually don't like to get to school this early."

"I want to meet with Sarah Harper before school," said Charlie.

Dad smiled and pointed to a bag of groceries in the front seat. "I'm making a special meal just for Mrs. Harper today. I'll show her that there's no need to order from Café Francois."

Charlie helped his dad carry the groceries to the cafeteria and then headed straight for the office. "Mr. Bacon, to what do I owe this privilege?" asked Mrs.

Simmons, the office manager, when he walked in.

"I'm looking for Sarah Harper," said Charlie.

"She certainly is popular this morning," said Mrs. Simmons. "You'll find her in the library."

Charlie hustled down the hall to the library. Sarah Harper was sitting at a table. The line of kids waiting to talk to her stretched all the way across the room. Allison was third in line. She was holding a life-size self-portrait.

Charlie made a beeline for Allison. He knew she would hog all the time if he didn't stop her. "Can I have your spot?" asked Charlie.

"Let me think about it," said Allison. "No. No way. No how. Go to the back of the line."

Sarah Harper looked up when she heard Allison's outburst. She smiled and said, "Good morning, Charlie Bacon."

Charlie felt his face flush red. She remembered his name. "Good morning," he said with a crooked smile.

"No line cuts," shouted a fifth grader.

Charlie took his place at the end of the line behind a tiny second grader. He watched the clock as the line slowly progressed. He was two students away from the table when the morning bell rang.

Charlie turned around and started to leave when he heard Sarah Harper's voice. "Can I walk you to class?" she asked.

"Of course," said Charlie. He felt like a celebrity as they walked down the hall to Room 7.

"What did you want to talk about?" asked Sarah.

"I'm stumped," confessed Charlie. "I can't decide what to make for the art show. I thought you might have an idea."

Sarah Harper smiled. "The best art comes from the

heart."

"My heart is blank," said Charlie.

Sarah Harper stopped walking. "You need a muse," she said.

"What's that?" asked Charlie.

"A muse is a person who inspires you artistically," explained Mrs. Harper. "It's different for every artist. My daughter Emily has been a great source of inspiration for my work. She's my muse. When you find your muse, you'll find your inspiration."

Charlie's face brightened into a smile. "I just need a muse," he said.

"That's right," said Sarah Harper. She turned around and was heading for the office when Charlie stopped her.

"My Uncle Mike has really bad gas too. I mean sometimes he sounds like a broken motorboat. He says a spoonful of baking soda helps with the problem. You might want to try it," said Charlie.

Mrs. Harper looked confused. She walked back to Charlie. "Excuse me, but do you think I have an issue with flatulence?"

"Dad says you're artsy-fartsy," confessed Charlie.

Mrs. Harper looked surprised and said, "He did, did he?"

"Yes, but between me and you, he's kind of fartsy himself sometimes," said Charlie.

"Charlie, the term artsy-fartsy does not refer to a person's flatulence. It means your father does not take me seriously as an artist. He thinks of me as some kind of fool," said Sarah.

"I don't think so," said Charlie. "He's going to make you your own special lunch today. He thinks you don't like his cooking."

"Does your father work in a restaurant?" asked Mrs. Harper.

"He's Chef Jeff, the school's cook," said Charlie. "You refused to eat his smack and cheese yesterday."

Sarah's face softened and she said, "OK, Charlie, you find your muse and I'll deal with your father."

Charlie began his search for a muse with his teacher. He stood in front of Mr. Beecher's desk and stared at him.

"Can I help you?" asked Mr. Beecher.

"I'm seeing if you inspire me," answered Charlie.

Mr. Beecher stared back at Charlie without speaking. After a long, uncomfortable minute Charlie said, "Nope." He scratched Mr. Beecher's name off his list.

Charlie then went down the rows of desks stopping at each student to see if anyone inspired him. Rhonda raised her hand. "Mr. Beecher, Charlie is creeping everyone out. He's acting very strange," she said.

"I agree," said Mr. Beecher. "Charlie, what is this all about?"

"I'm trying to find my muse," said Charlie, moving to Tony's desk.

"I don't have it," said Tony. "I think Rayce took it."

"I did not," snapped Rayce.

"Charlie, go to your seat," said Mr. Beecher. Charlie sat down at his desk.

"What is a muse?" asked Rhonda.

"A muse is a person who provides inspiration for an artist," explained Mr. Beecher.

"Like me," said Allison. "I inspire lots of people. I'll be your muse, Charlie Bacon."

"Let me think about it," said Charlie. "No. No way. No how. Go to the back of the line."

Allison folded her arms and stuck her tongue out at Charlie. By the time the afternoon bell rang, he was still uninspired.

Chapter 6

Best Ride Ever!

"Do you want to go sledding this afternoon?" asked Biff as they walked home. "My brother Zany has built a super sleigh called the No Noggin Toboggan. He says it will blow every other sled off the planet. He's looking for a couple of test pilots."

"It sounds dangerous," said Charlie. "Of course, I'm in."

"Good, because I already told him we'd do it. We're going to test it on Gravity Hill this afternoon," said Biff.

"Why doesn't Zany ride it?" asked Charlie.

"If we survive he's going to try and set a world land

speed record," explained Biff.

Charlie hurried home and announced to his mother, "I need to go to Biff's house. It's real important. I won't stay all afternoon. And yes, I will do my homework when I get home."

"Are you trying to read my mind by answering my questions before I ask them?" asked Mom.

"I guess," said Charlie.

Mom wrinkled her brow and asked, "What am I thinking now?"

Charlie squinted as he looked at Mom and replied, "You're the best son in the universe, so go and have fun."

"Close enough," said Mom. She kissed Charlie's forehead and he hurried out the door.

Biff and Zany were waiting in their front yard when Charlie arrived. Zany was wearing an old-fashioned motorcycle helmet and a shiny white daredevil jumpsuit. It was decorated with yellow lightning bolts and red stars. A bright blue cape was tied around his skinny neck.

"Halloween is over," teased Charlie.

Zany smacked Charlie on the back of the head and said, "I'm a daredevil. Today is the day I ride the No Noggin Toboggan into fame and glory. But bravery is something you know nothing about."

"I thought we were going to ride the No Noggin Toboggan," said Charlie.

"You are," said Zany. "And if it doesn't kill you then I'll ride it."

"What's that?" asked Charlie, pointing to a car hood in the front yard.

"That, my uneducated little friend, is the No Noggin Toboggan. The fastest sled ever invented," replied Zany. "The car it came off of was a sports car that could go faster than 120 miles per hour. Without the rest of the car slowing it down, I think the hood will go even faster. Grab that rope and help me pull it to Gravity Hill."

Biff and Charlie took hold of the rope and pulled while Zany sat on the sled. "This would be easier if you'd get off and walk. We're not sled dogs," complained Biff.

"Hush and mush," snapped Zany.

"Where did Zany get the daredevil suit?" asked Charlie.

"It's not real," whispered Biff. "Mr. Crackles, our neighbor across the street, used to be a professional clown. He has all kinds of costumes and props. When Zany told me his idea, I borrowed the costume. It's a trick suit that has a rip cord that makes the whole thing come apart."

"Does Zany know that?" asked Charlie.

"I may have forgotten to mention it," said Biff, smiling.

Gravity Hill was at the end of Biff's neighborhood.

It had a gradual slope at first but then dropped almost straight down before leveling off again. It ended at the fence that bordered Central Elementary.

There were a lot of kids already sledding when the boys arrived. "It looks like you're going to have a big audience," said Biff.

"I should charge admission," said Zany. "These nincompoops are going to witness history today."

Charlie and Biff pushed the No Noggin Toboggan to the edge of the hill. "You need to understand this is no ordinary sled," explained Zany. "You can't steer it and it has no brakes. You idiots, I mean you guys, make the first run. If you survive, I'll take the second run."

Biff and Charlie flopped onto the makeshift sled, belly first. They gripped the front of the hood and looked down the hill.

"Are you ready?" asked Zany.

Biff gritted his teeth while Charlie yelled, "Let's go!"

Zany gave the hood a huge shove and they were off. The No Noggin Toboggan was a speed demon. Both boys howled like maniacs as they rocketed down Gravity Hill.

"Abandon ship! We'll never stop before the fence," yelled Charlie when they hit the open field. Biff and Charlie rolled off the sled and tumbled in the soft snow. The No Noggin Toboggan crashed full speed into the chain-link fence.

The boys jumped up screaming. "That was awesome!" yelled Biff.

"I can't believe we're alive," shouted Charlie.

They jerked the toboggan away from the fence and pulled it up the hill to where Zany was waiting. "How was it?" he asked excitedly.

"Best ride ever!" shouted Charlie.

"A thousand times better than a roller coaster," added Biff. "You're going to love it."

Zany stood on the hood. "I'm going surfer style," he said. He reached into a pocket and pulled out his phone. Handing it to Charlie he said, "Get a picture of me coming down the hill. If it's as good as I think it'll be, it will go viral on the Internet."

Charlie slid down the hill to get in a position to take a picture while Biff pushed the sled to the starting point. Biff yelled, "Yeehaw," and pushed the sled over the edge. As the No Noggin Toboggan headed down the hill Biff grabbed the rip cord on the back of the daredevil costume. The colorful suit flew off Zany's skinny body and fell to the ground. Wearing only snow boots, underwear, and the blue cape, Zany rocketed down the hill.

Charlie and Biff cheered as Zany surfed down the hill. The No Noggin Toboggan was going full speed when it hit the fence. The crash launched Zany into the air. Like a flying superhero, his blue cape fluttered in the wind as he flew over the fence and belly-flopped onto the school's playground.

Zany was still facedown in the snow when Biff and Charlie got to him. "You did it," shouted Biff. "You went so fast you flew right out of your clothes."

Charlie was still taking pictures when Zany finally got to his feet. He walked like a frozen zombie up the hill and straight home.

"Do you think he's all right?" asked Charlie. "It's not like him to have nothing to say."

"He'll have plenty to say when he thaws out," said Biff. "Let's get the sled and take the daredevil suit back to Bob Crackles."

Chapter 7

Outside the Box

"Check out this doorbell," said Biff, squeezing the bright red bubble of a clown horn. After the third honk, the door flew open. Bob Crackles was a squatty man with bushy red eyebrows.

"How did the suit work?" he asked.

"Hilarious," said Biff.

"Who's your friend?" asked Bob when he spotted Charlie.

"This is Charlie Bacon," said Biff. "He's my best friend."

"Nice to meet you," said Bob Crackles, extending his hand to Charlie.

When Charlie shook Bob's hand, he let out a howl. Bob laughed and showed the boys the palm of his hand. "Hand buzzer, gets them every time."

Charlie looked into the living room and said, "Wow." The room was stacked floor to ceiling with clown supplies. From squirting flowers to whoopee cushions, there was every trick and joke imaginable.

"Come have a look," said Bob. "After thirty years in the clown biz, you collect a few things."

Charlie walked slowly as he tried to get a look at everything. Beneath a shelf full of fake noses was a large suitcase. "What's in that?" he asked.

"This is the world's largest briefcase." boasted Bob. He opened it and pulled out a humongous pair of underwear. "And these are the world's largest pair of briefs. Get it?"

"Tighty-whities," said Charlie, laughing.

"They're not tighty-whities. They're loosey-gooseys," joked Bob.

Charlie and Biff were trying on clown noses and crazy wigs when music erupted in Charlie's pocket. "That's Zany's ringtone," said Biff. "You must still have his phone."

Charlie took out the phone and handed it to Biff who answered it. "Hello." The voice on the other end was high-pitched and screaming.

"We are not trying to steal your phone," explained Biff. "I'm on my way home."

Biff touched the hang-up button and said, "We've got to go. Zany's having a meltdown." Before they left, Biff opened the pictures folder so they could show Bob the pictures of Zany's wild ride. Bob Crackles took the phone and studied a close-up picture of Zany's face.

"Interesting," he said. "When I was with the circus I

worked with lots of daredevils. They all had one thing in common."

"No brains?" guessed Charlie.

"Courage," said Bob. "You could always see it in their eyes. Your brother doesn't look scared. He looks brave."

"Where there is courage there is hope," whispered Charlie to himself.

"What'd you say?" asked Bob.

"Where there is courage, there is hope," repeated Charlie. "It's something my grandma always says."

"That's very profound," said Bob.

Suddenly, Charlie's eyes widened and he blurted, "I've got it. If I can capture the courage of Zany's ride in art, I'm sure to win Best of Show."

"You're going to paint a picture of Zany?" asked Biff.

"Nope," said Charlie. "I'm going to make a magnificent snow sculpture. I'll call him Wil-burrr the Eighth Wonder of the Universe."

"Sounds great," said Biff.

"You haven't even heard the best part," said Charlie. "He'll be wearing the world's largest pair of underpants. What about it, Mr. Crackles? Can I borrow the loosey-gooseys?"

"Of course," said Bob handing Charlie the briefs.

Charlie stopped at Biff's house to get the helmet and cape before hurrying home to work on the Eighth Wonder of the Universe. He was still rolling the first snowball for his snowman when his mom called him in for supper. "Just five more minutes," begged Charlie. "I'm working on something big."

"It can wait," said Mom as she closed the door.

Dad served vegetable lasagna and garlic bread

for supper. It was Charlie's favorite meal. "Can I have seconds?" asked Charlie after devouring his first serving.

"Of course," said Dad, grinning. He scooped another serving of lasagna onto Charlie's plate.

Mom turned to Charlie and asked, "So what are you making in the backyard?"

"I'll show you," said Charlie, jumping up from the table. He raced into his room and returned with the world's largest pair of underwear.

"Sick," said Shrudi. "Get those away from the food."

"They're clean," said Charlie. "I'm creating a snow statue for the art show, and he's going to wear these."

"Underpants on a snowman is the dumbest idea I've ever heard of," said Shrudi. "Why don't you just draw a picture like everyone else?"

"Because he's an artist just like his father," said

Dad. "Like all great artists, we think outside of the box. Charlie creates with snow and I create with food. After tasting my cooking, Sarah Harper has personally requested that I create the desserts for the art show."

Charlie's little brother, Jimmy, interrupted the conversation by throwing a lasagna noodle at Charlie. The saucy pasta slid down Charlie's forehead before landing on the floor.

Jimmy laughed and reached for a second noodle. "It seems Jimmy thinks outside the box too," said Mom, getting up from the table. "Come on, Shrudi, let's leave these great artists to their work."

"But it's girls' night to do the dishes," complained Charlie.

"Think outside the box," said Mom, leaving the room.

Chapter 8
Building a Masterpiece

Sarah Harper showed up at Room 7 right after morning recess. "There are only two days until the Celebration of Inspiration," she announced. "I hope you've all been working on your art pieces. This is the last time we'll meet before the art show."

Allison raised her hand. "Can I be one of the judges?" she blurted before Mrs. Harper could call on her.

"Dr. Brown, Mrs. Simmons, and I will be the judges," replied Sarah Harper.

"Can I enter more than one painting?" asked Allison.

"No, the rules are clear," said Mrs. Harper.

"No more questions," said Mr. Beecher.

"Remember this is a high-class event," explained Mrs. Harper. "I hope you wear best dress. That means button shirts and ties for the gentlemen and dresses or slacks for the ladies. Today I will conference with each of you at the front table where we'll briefly discuss your art piece."

Charlie looked around the room. He was the only one without any art. There were paintings, drawings, and sculptures made out of building blocks, wax, and clay. Charlie tore a piece of paper out of his notebook and quickly sketched the Eighth Wonder of the Universe.

When it was his turn, Charlie hurried to the table and took a seat across from his favorite artist. "Hello, Mr. Bacon," said Mrs. Harper with a huge smile. "Did you find your muse?"

"I hope so," said Charlie. "I'm creating the Eighth Wonder of the Universe, but it's too big to bring to class."

"Well, can you tell me about it?" asked Mrs. Harper. Charlie showed her the sketch of Wil-burrr.

"Interesting," said Mrs. Harper. "Is this a snowman?"

"A gigantic one, like one of Michelangelo's statues," explained Charlie.

"Is he wearing enormous underpants?" asked Mrs. Harper.

"Yes, I borrowed them from a clown," explained Charlie.

Sarah Harper furrowed her brow and thought for a moment. "How are you going to get something this big to school?" she asked.

"I'm building it on a huge sled and I'm going to pull it to school," said Charlie. "Can you judge him outside? If I bring him in the school he'll melt."

"Of course," said Mrs. Harper. "Did your father tell you he's making the desserts for the show?"

"Oh yeah," said Charlie. "He's real excited about it."

"Wonderful, he really is a delightful chef. I'm sorry I didn't eat his food the first day. It had more to do with me trying to lose a few pounds than with his cooking," explained Sara Harper, holding her hand out to Charlie.

"I'm glad you don't have a terrible gas problem," said Charlie, shaking her hand.

"Good luck, Charlie Bacon," said Sarah Harper, as Charlie returned to his seat.

Charlie couldn't wait to get back to work on his masterpiece. He raced straight home from school. After checking in with Mom, he hurried to the backyard and began rolling Wil-burrr's bottom around the yard. As the snow collected, it became harder and harder to roll.

Charlie positioned the underpants in the middle of the No Noggin Toboggan. He rolled the huge ball of snow until it was centered in the underwear. Grabbing the elastic waistband he gave a hard yank and the underwear popped up over the top of the snowball.

Wil-burrr was in his tighty-whities. Charlie gave an extra tug and the underpants crept up higher. "Uh oh," said Charlie, laughing. "Almost gave you a wedgie."

The back door opened and out dashed the family's dachshund, Oscar. He disappeared in the fluffy snow like a wiener dog submarine. He surfaced again next to the No Noggin Toboggan.

"Don't even think about it," warned Charlie. "Go do your business somewhere else." Oscar bounded over to the flower bed where he made some yellow snow.

Charlie went straight to work on Wil-burrr's midsection. He rolled the ball until it was so big his arms couldn't reach around it. He pushed it over to the sled and tried to heave it on top of the bottom ball. It was too heavy.

Oscar was waiting at the door to be let back in

when Charlie dashed in the house to look for help. He found Shrudi doing her homework. "Will you help me for a minute?" asked Charlie.

"Do I look like your servant?" asked Shrudi.

Charlie wanted to say, "yes" but decided to sweet talk her instead. "Have I ever told you that you're the best sis. . ."

Shrudi held her hand up to stop him mid-sentence. "You're wasting your breath. I'm not getting off this couch."

Charlie found Mom coming out of Jimmy's room. She shushed Charlie and whispered, "I just got Jimmy down for his nap. What do you want?"

"Can you help me with my snowman?" he softly asked.

"I'd love to," said Mom. "Give me a second to get my coat and gloves."

While Charlie waited he made a couple of snow angels. Mom fell backward in the snow to make one of her own. "These always make me think of Grandma," said Charlie. "Do you think she'll come to the art show?"

"She said she would," said Mom. Charlie smiled and made his angel extra big.

With Mom's help Charlie completed Wil-burrr's body. Together they broke off some branches for his arms. Radish eyes, a carrot nose and a banana smile completed Wil-burrr's face. Mom placed the helmet on Wil-burrr's head and tied the cape around his neck.

They stood back and admired their work. "I think Wilburrr has been working out at the gym. He's buff," said Mom, laughing.

"Do you think he looks brave?" asked Charlie.

"He's the bravest snowman I've ever seen," answered Mom.

Chapter 9

The Atomic
Wedgie

Charlie looked at himself in the mirror as he got ready for the Celebration of Inspiration. He was wearing the cherry red bow tie that Great-Aunt Wanda had given him for his birthday and his white button-down shirt.

"Get out of the bathroom," ordered Shrudi. "You've been in there all afternoon."

"I'm grooming," said Charlie, leaning back to inspect his nostrils in the mirror.

"If you're using my toothbrush again, I will make sure you go to jail for it," shouted Shrudi, pounding on the door.

"Is your toothbrush the pink one?" asked Charlie. "I accidently used it to clean the toilet."

Shrudi banged on the door harder. "You're supposed to go get Oscar. He's outside doing his business."

"You do it," said Charlie.

"I have to get ready to go to your ridiculous art show," said Shrudi.

Charlie opened the door and said, "It's all yours."

"What's that horrific smell?" asked Shrudi as she pushed past Charlie.

"That's the smell of success," said Charlie. He put on his boots and coat and hurried out the back door.

When Charlie spotted Oscar standing next to Wilburrr his heart began to race. He sprinted over to the snowman and shouted, "Bad dog! Bad dog! Bad dog!" The Eighth Wonder of the Universe had just been peed on by the Eighth Weirdest Dog in the Universe.

Charlie swooped Oscar up in his arms and marched into the house. "Do I have permission to ship Oscar to China?" yelled Charlie.

"What's going on?" asked Mom.

"The dumb dog whizzed on Wil-burrr," snapped Charlie. "He ruined my masterpiece."

"Calm down," said Mom. "Luckily, Oscar is short, so the stain has to be near the bottom. Maybe no one will notice."

"It is yellow snow," blurted Charlie. "Everyone's going to notice."

"You're going to have to dig out the yellow snow and fill in the hole with fresh snow," said Mom. "But hurry, you don't have much time."

Charlie raced into the kitchen and pulled open the utensil drawer. He grabbed the salad tongs and a carving knife. He rushed to the scene of the accident to perform emergency surgery.

Dr. Bacon examined the wound. It was much bigger than he first thought. "How can one little dog pee so much?" asked Charlie to himself. "This is going to be major surgery."

He picked up the knife. "This might sting a little," he said to the patient. He shoved the knife deep into the yellow snow and loosened a large chunk. Using the salad tongs he removed the first glob of yellow snow.

Charlie was still operating when Mom arrived to assist. "Are those my salad tongs?" she asked.

"Shhh," hushed Charlie. "This is a delicate operation." He dropped the tongs and picked up the knife to dig deeper into the side of the snowman.

"You're taking out a lot of snow," said Mom. "I better hold on to Wil-burrr in case he begins to tip."

"Good idea," said Dr. Bacon as he dug deeper into the base of the snowman. Mom circled to the back of Wil-burrr and slid her fingers under the waistband of his underwear. She got a good grip and held tight.

"Did I ever tell you that your Uncle Mike used to give the worst wedgies on the planet? He called them atomic wedgies," said Mom. "He'd sneak up behind someone and before they knew what was happening, he'd grab the top of their unders and yank for all he was worth. Just like this." Charlie's mom tugged as hard as she could on Wil-burrr's tighty-whities.

In his weakened condition, the atomic wedgie was more than Wil-burrr could handle. He teetered and tottered and tipped over, landing right on top of Dr. Bacon. Charlie disappeared beneath the gigantic snowman.

Mom attacked Wil-burrr like a ninja. She hit,

shoved, and dug through his frozen body to free her son. By the time she got to Charlie, the snow sculpture was totally destroyed.

"Are you all right?" asked Mom.

Charlie sat up and hugged his mom. "That was scary," he said. "Is Wil-burrr OK?"

"Honey, I've got some bad news," said Mom, holding Charlie tight. "Your snowman didn't survive the accident. He's gone to the big snowdrift in the sky."

Charlie wiggled free and looked at the snow chunks that used to be his masterpiece. His eyes widened and he asked, "Did you give Wil-burrr a wedgie?"

"I may have given his unders a little tug," confessed Mom.

"That wedgie killed my snowman," accused Charlie.

"Honey, I'm sorry," said Mom. "Maybe we can hurry and put him back together."

"There's not enough time," said Charlie, fighting back tears. "I'm just going to stay home."

"I know you're disappointed and you have every right to be," said Mom. "This is one of those times when you have to be brave. Your friends need your support. Dad has made some fancy French desserts. And Grandma's going to be there just for you."

Charlie shrugged and mumbled, "OK, I'll go but I won't enjoy it."

Chapter 10
Angel Heart

The air was full of excitement when Charlie walked into Central Elementary. A string quartet was playing classical music at one end of the multipurpose room. Charlie's dad was serving fancy cookies and fruit punch at the other end. The center of the room was lined with tables loaded with paintings and sculptures.

The students were standing next to their art creations while the parents and judges came by. Biff was standing next to a duck made out of duct tape.

"Nice duck," said Charlie.

"It's Doug the Duct Tape Duck," explained Biff. "I just covered one of my Dad's hunting decoys with duct

tape. How's Wil-burrr?"

"He was killed by a giant wedgie," said Charlie.

"I know how that feels," said Biff. "Zany is the king of wedgies."

Charlie hurried over to his dad to get some goodies. "This is a delicious cookie," said Charlie.

"It's a petit four," said Dad in a phony French accent. "Did you have any trouble getting your statue here?"

"Mom destroyed it before we even left home," said Charlie.

Dad dropped the phony accent and asked, "What happened?"

"I was cleaning the pee off Wil-burrr when Mom gave him a wedgie and he tipped over on me. Mom went mental and ripped him to shreds. That's pretty much it," explained Charlie.

"Sounds horrible," said Dad. "You better have another petit four and some fruit punch."

Charlie grabbed another cookie and spotted Grandma coming though the door. He hurried over to meet her.

"Who's this handsome fellow?" asked Grandma when she caught a glimpse of Charlie.

"Hi, Grandma," said Charlie smiling. Suddenly, he felt better.

"Where's this masterpiece I've heard so much about?" asked Grandma. Charlie's smile faded and he explained the tragedy.

"Maybe it's not too late to whip something together. Where there is courage, there is hope," said Grandma.

"Not this time," said Charlie. "It would take a miracle and I don't see any angels around here waiting to help."

Grandma smiled and said, "I'll help."

Charlie looked at his grandma's smile and felt hopeful. He felt more than hopeful. He felt inspired. Suddenly, it was clear who his muse was and he knew exactly what he wanted to do.

"Grab your coat," said Charlie excitedly. "We've got work to do."

They zipped out the double doors that led to the playground. The ground was covered with freshly

fallen snow. Charlie tiptoed through the snow to a large open area. He fell on his back and made a snow angel.

"What should I do?" asked Grandma.

"Make another angel so that our two angels form a V," explained Charlie. Grandma tiptoed over and made a snow angel. Charlie stood up and made another snow angel above the first one. "Copy my moves," he said.

When they were done, Charlie and Grandma had made a giant heart out of snow angels. "It's an angel heart," said Grandma, beaming.

Charlie jumped in the center of the heart and wrote, "Be Brave" in huge letters. He tiptoed back out of the heart and stood next to Grandma.

"It's amazing," said Grandma.

Charlie dashed back into the school and found Mrs. Harper, who was talking to a group of students."Is it too late to be judged?" he asked.

"Your father told me that Wil-burrr didn't make the trip," said Mrs. Harper.

"He's right," said Charlie. "But I've got something better. It's outside by the playground."

Dr. Brown came over to Mrs. Harper. "I think we've got it all sorted out," he said. "I'm ready to announce the winners."

"There's one late entry," said Mrs. Harper. "We need to go outside to see it."

"We've already made our choices," argued Dr. Brown.

Sarah Harper looked at Charlie and said, "I'm sorry, Charlie. Dr. Brown is right."

Charlie looked over at Grandma, who gave him an encouraging smile. "You don't have to judge it. Just come and look at it," he pleaded. "It will just take a minute."

"OK, let's go," said Mrs. Harper. "Dr. Brown, I'll be right back."

Sarah Harper followed Charlie. A large group of students followed both of them. When they got to the playground, Charlie announced. "I give to you the Ninth Wonder of the Universe, Angel Heart."

Sarah's smile seemed to take up her entire face. "Is it art?" asked Charlie.

"Before Mrs. Harper could answer, a first grader plopped down in the fresh snow and called out, "I'm brave," as she made a snow angel.

She was followed by three more students who fell in the snow and called out, "I'm brave," while making snow angels.

Those three were followed by five more, who were followed by ten more. Soon parents and students were coming out of the school to see what the commotion was about. They joined in and snow angels filled the playground while shouts of "I'm brave," filled the air.

Sarah Harper crowned her snow angel with an artistic halo before singing, "I'm brave." She looked over at Dr. Brown who was standing in the doorway with his hands on his hips.

"Come on, Dr. Brown, be brave," called out Mrs. Harper.

The principal made a quick angel before announcing, "Everyone back in the school. We're ready to hand out the awards."

Back in the school, Dr. Brown stood at a podium next to a table that held a stack of ribbons. He announced grade level winners for best drawing, painting, and sculpture. Ronnie Wilkins, a fifth grader, won Best in Show for a painting of his grandfather.

After Ronnie sat down, Sarah Harper whispered

something to Dr. Brown. He nodded and announced, "I've just been informed that there is one more award. The award for Best in Snow goes to Charlie Bacon."

Students began to shout, "I'm brave," as Charlie made his way to the front of the room. Sarah Harper presented him with an autographed print of Taj the elephant. At the bottom of the picture she had written, "To Charlie Bacon, where there is courage, there is hope. Best Wishes, Sarah Harper."

When the family got home, Charlie walked over to the remains of Wil-burrr. He reached down and formed a snowball. He took aim at Shrudi and let the ball fly. At that moment Shrudi moved and the snowball hit Mom in the head.

Mom reached down to grab some snow and Shrudi yelled, "Run, Charlie! Run!"

About the Author

Gary Hogg is the author of more than twenty books. His hilarious stories include *Look What the Cat Dragged In*, *I Heard of a Nerd Bird*, and the popular *Spencer's Adventures* series. Gary says his fourth grade teacher inspired him to put his wild ideas into stories instead of acting them out in class. She kept her sanity and he became a writer. Of all the characters he's created, Gary says Charlie Bacon is the most like him.

Gary is a popular speaker and guest author. He has inspired over 2 million students to be better writers with his popular *Writing is Exciting!* assembly and workshop program. You can learn about him at **www.garyhoggbooks.com**.